The Loch MESS Monster

Written by Helen Lester

Illustrated by Lynn Munsinger

To my husband, Robin, and (at the risk of being tacky) to his novel,
Princes of New York. — H.L.

GLOSSARY of SCOTTISH TERMS
(in order of appearance)

loch	lake
wee laddie	little boy
skirps	drips
puggy-nit	peanut
hummie-doddies	mittens
grottie	dirty
tatties	potatoes
Heeland coo	Highland cow
peelie-wallie	sick

This paperback first published in Great Britain in 2014 by Andersen Press Ltd.,
20 Vauxhall Bridge Road, London SW1V 2SA.

Published in Australia by Random House Australia Pty., Level 3, 100 Pacific Highway, North Sydney, NSW 2060.
Text copyright © 2014 Helen Lester. Illustration copyright © 2014 Lynn Munsinger.

Published by special arrangement with Houghton Mifflin Harcourt Publishing Company, and Rights People, London.
The rights of Helen Lester and Lynn Munsinger to be identified as the author and illustrator
of this work have been asserted by them in accordance with the Copyright, Designs and Patents Act, 1988.
All rights reserved. Colour separated in Switzerland by Photolitho AG, Zürich.
Printed and bound in Singapore by Tien Wah Press.

10   9   8   7   6   5   4   3   2   1

British Library Cataloguing in Publication Data available.

ISBN 978 1 78344 154 9

In faraway Scotland there was a famous lake called Loch Ness.
And legend had it that deep in this lake lived a monster.
No one had ever seen it.

But guess what? The legend was false.

In truth, way, way down at the bottom
of Loch Ness there lived not one . . .

but *three* monsters!

There was Nessie, her husband, Fergus, and their wee laddie,

Angus.

From the time he was a baby, Angus's parents had taught him the Five Basic Monster Rules.

Five Basic Monster Rules

#5. Never behave in a monstrous manner.

#4. Never eat with your thumbs.

#3. Always say "Excuse me" when you cough, sneeze, or burp.

#2. Always pick up after yourself.

#1. Never ever EVER go up to the surface of the loch.

So Angus was well behaved, ate with a spoon, and said "Excuse me" when he coughed, sneezed, or burped.

But as he grew bigger, so did his messes.

Mother Nessie skidded across the floor on Angus's slimy lochweed collection and crashed into Father Fergus.

Father Fergus tripped over Angus's fishy dolls and landed in the porridge.

Angus loved the action. His parents did not.

"Have you noticed that our laddie leaves skirps all over his dishes?" they asked.

"And puggy-nit shells on the floor?"

"And that his hummie-doddies are hopelessly mixed up?"

"And that we're surrounded by grottie laundry?"

What had happened to their tidy home?
ANGUS had happened.

It was time to enforce Basic Monster Rule #2:
Always pick up after yourself.

So Angus's parents told him that while they loved him very much, until he cleaned up after himself he would have to stay in his room so that his stuff would stop spreading.

Meanwhile, they would deliver his daily meal of milk and tatties-in-a-can. So Angus went off to his room.

In the days that followed he didn't feel lonesome, for he had so much interesting stuff.

Every day he would play with his toys, tossing each one on the floor when he had finished.

Before long the floor was full.
So Angus tossed his used items onto the bed.

And a monstrously messy
mountain began to grow.

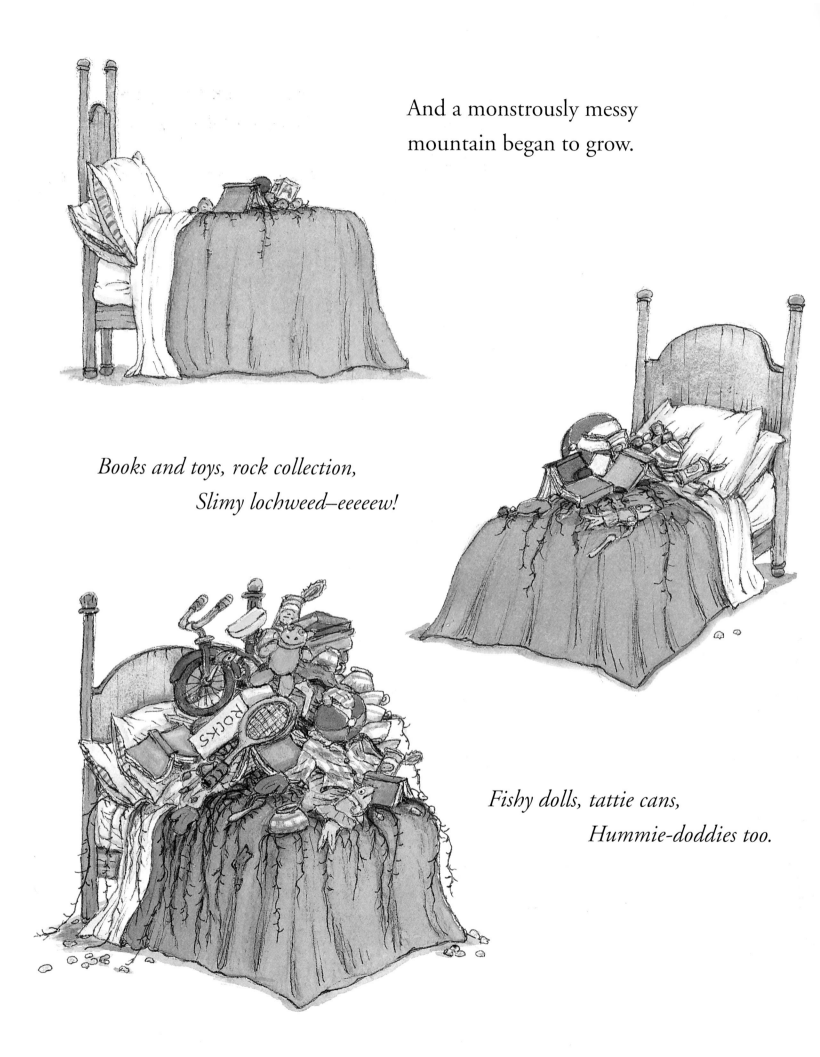

Books and toys, rock collection,
   Slimy lochweed–eeeeew!

Fishy dolls, tattie cans,
   Hummie-doddies too.

Grottie laundry, puggy-nits,
Spoon and skirpy cup–

Messy mountain moving higher,
Up and up and up.

At night, as was his habit, Angus would check to be sure there were no monsters under the bed.

Then he would strap on his mountain gear and make the long climb to his lumpy sleeping perch.

Each night this climb took a little longer,
because each day he added:

> Books and toys, rock collection,
> Slimy lochweed–eeeeew!
> Fishy dolls, tattie cans,
> Hummie-doddies too.
> Grottie laundry, puggy-nits,
> Spoon and skirpy cup–
> Messy mountain moving higher,
> Up and up and up.

Not only was the climb a long way up.

On the nights when Angus fell out of bed, it was a

lonnnnnng

waaaaaaaaay

down!

Now Angus was beginning to miss his parents.

He was uncomfortable on his lumpy bed, and dreadfully hot
as he neared the sun on the surface of the loch.

Surface of the loch . . . Angus had forgotten Basic
Monster Rule #1: *NevereverEVER go up to the surface of the loch.*

But here was Angus. Rising.

Meanwhile, three friends gathered on the shores of Loch Ness.
A duck, a goat, and a Heeland coo looked out over the water as they
had every morning for years, waiting patiently for the Loch Ness
monster to appear.

And at last on this particular morning they saw a wee ripple way out on the loch. Could it possibly be? They focused their camera, binoculars, and telescope, and what they saw was . . .

Sloppy Angus, just awakening and rising on his bed, or what once had been his bed.

"WHAT A MESS!" exclaimed the three observers.

The trio sadly shook their heads.

"It's nae the Loch Ness Monster.

'Tis the Loch MESS Monster."

And what did Angus see on the shore? What he saw made him feel absolutely peelie-wallie! Monstrous land-monsters!

The little one had enormous feet that could
probably stomp you flat in a second.
The middle one had a hairy chin, fierce spears
on its noggin, and big, googly eyes.
And the big one must have been five
hundred feet tall, with a long green snout.
And it made the most horrible sound–
MOOOOMOOOO-
MOOOOOOOOOOOOOOO.

Time to moooooooove! Suddenly, Sloppy Angus wanted to clean up!
He gathered up as much stuff as his arms could hold and climbed down,
down, down to the bottom of his mountain.

"Let's see . . . slimy lochweed on the shelf, puggy-nit shells in the laundry basket, books and toys in the bin, grottie laundry in the fish tank . . ."

No. Wait. That wasn't right.
Slimy lochweed in the fish tank, grottie laundry in the basket, puggy-nit shells in the bin, books and toys on the shelf—

NOW Angus remembered!

And up, up he went for another load.

Up and down

and up and down,

load after load, until at last all of his stuff had found a place.

Books and toys, rock collection,
Slimy lochweed—eeeeew!
Fishy dolls, tattie cans,
Hummie-doddies too.
Grottie laundry, puggy-nits,
Spoon and skirpy cup—
Messy mountain is no more—
Angus cleaned it up!

Angus was thrilled to see his parents, and as he passed them he called cheerfully, "I'm off to wash my dishes and recycle my tatties-in-a-can cans."

His mother and father were concerned.

"Are ye peelie-wallie, laddie?"

But Angus was not peelie-wallie. He was just glad to be plain Angus instead of Sloppy Angus.

That night he had a wonderful dinner with his parents,
and land-monster-free dreams on his smooth, cool bed.

EPILOGUE

But Angus didn't want his parents to think he was perfect, so once in a while he acted a little bit monstrous and left a . . .

. . . very wee mess.